SIMON SOCK

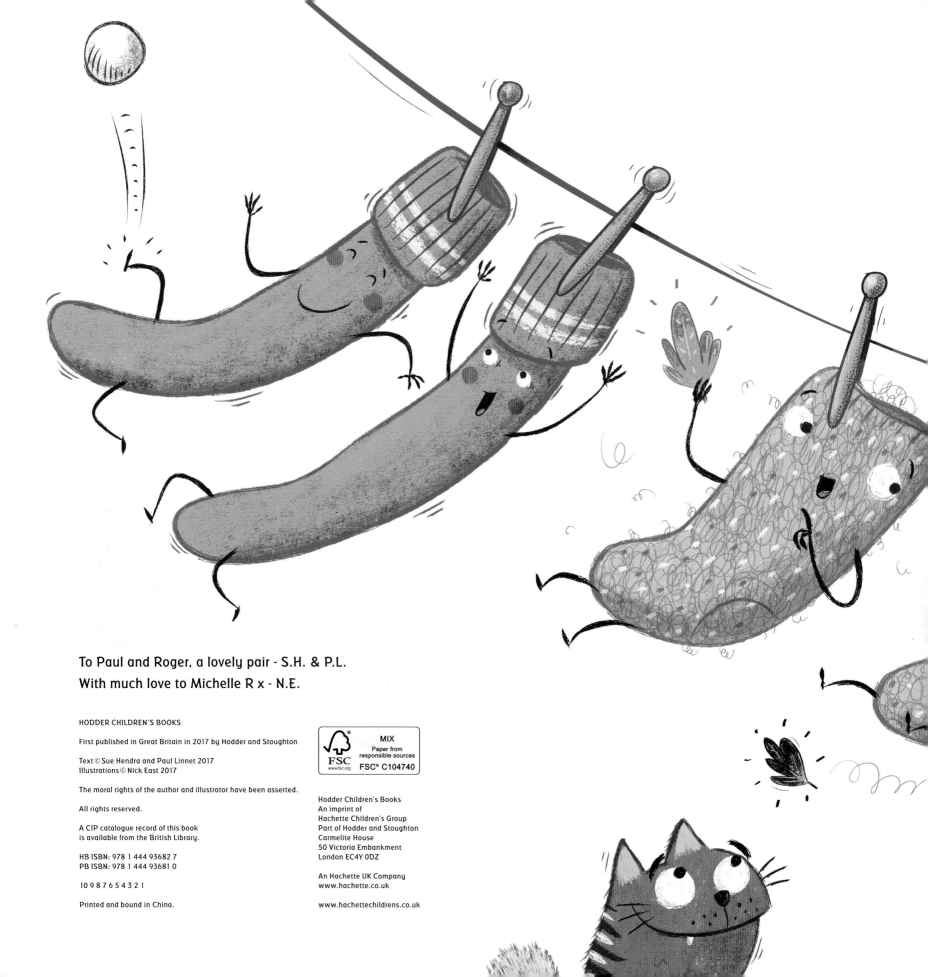

To Paul and Roger, a lovely pair - S.H. & P.L.
With much love to Michelle R x - N.E.

HODDER CHILDREN'S BOOKS

First published in Great Britain in 2017 by Hodder and Stoughton

Text © Sue Hendra and Paul Linnet 2017
Illustrations © Nick East 2017

The moral rights of the author and illustrator have been asserted.

A CIP catalogue record of this book
is available from the British Library.

HB ISBN: 978 1 444 93682 7
PB ISBN: 978 1 444 93681 0

10 9 8 7 6 5 4 3 2 1

Printed and bound in China.

MIX
Paper from
responsible sources
FSC® C104740
FSC
www.fsc.org

Hodder Children's Books
An imprint of
Hachette Children's Group
Part of Hodder and Stoughton
Carmelite House
50 Victoria Embankment
London EC4Y 0DZ

An Hachette UK Company
www.hachette.co.uk

www.hachettechildrens.co.uk

SIMON SOCK

Written by Sue Hendra and Paul Linnet
Illustrated by Nick East

Hodder
Children's
Books

Simon is extremely stripy.
He lives in the sock drawer with all
the other socks. It's very cosy in there.

Every morning all the socks in the drawer get very excited. Who will it be today?

Then in comes the hand…

"Pick me! Pick me!"

Everybody waits, holding their breath…

...and two socks get
picked to go on
an adventure.

The sparklies go to parties!

The woollies go to the park.

The smarts go to school.

And the sporties go for the burn!
Ready, steady, GO!

Everyone has a turn.

Everyone except Simon.

"I'm not a smelly sock.

And I'm not a holey sock!

Why don't I ever have a turn?"

PICK ME

"Oh, I didn't realise I was odd," said Simon.
"Maybe the spotties are right.
If only I was a pair...

We could skate, we could bounce, we could hula!
We could have so much fun!" said Simon sadly.

"I've got it!" shouts Ted,
jumping to his feet.

POP

PICK
ME

"I've got a friend and he's stripy just like you, Simon!

Come on! He lives in the hall ...

"Simon, this is Alphonse. Alphonse, this is Simon."

And everything was going well…

...until in walked Petra.

"Oh, silly me," said Ted. "I forgot they were already a pair. Don't worry though, Simon, I have another stripy friend!"

"Simon, meet Shirley!" said Ted hopefully.

ssssssssssssssssss

Shirley was very excited, but
Simon was a little bit nervous.

SQUEEZE

"I'm not sure about this, Ted," said Simon.

"What about Desmond?" said Ted.
But Desmond just stared.

"He's not very chatty, is he?"
said Simon.

"No, not really," replied Ted,
"but we can't give up now.

I have lots of stripy friends. What about...

...Bobby?"

"But I can't swim!"
whispered Simon.

"Debra, the stripy bug?"

"She's very tiny, Ted.
I might step on her."

"What about Jeff?" said Ted.
"He's very musical..."

"He's very noisy!"

"Hatty?"

CHITTER CHATTER CHITTER
CHITTER CHATTER CHITTER

"Too chatty!"

"Trevor?"

"No way!"

"Well, you'll be pleased to know I've saved the best until last," said Ted proudly. "Simon, meet...

Simon had had enough.

"It's no good, Ted. I just need to get used to being an odd sock," he said sadly.

But then he heard a voice. It was coming from under the drawers…

"HELLO?"

Simon couldn't believe it.
"I've found you!" he cried.

"We're a pair!
We can skate!!
We can bounce!!!
We can hula!!!!"

"Come on," said Simon, "let's go out and play!"

But Simone had other ideas.

Betty gave Simon a wave.

Simon waved back.

"I like playing!" said Betty.

So they skated,

and they bounced,

and they hula hooped!

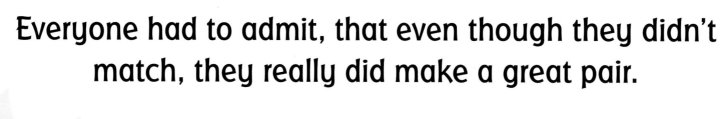

Everyone had to admit, that even though they didn't match, they really did make a great pair.